THE SHADOWLESS

THE DARK VEIL OPENS

by

Christopher D. Schmitz

the Shadowless: The Dark Veil Opens

the Shadowless: The Dark Veil Opens

Special Offer:

Stay up to date on the world of Shadowless. Join the author's no-spam newsletter and get freebies, exclusive content, and much more!

To join, simply visit this link:

https://www.subscribepage.com/shadowless

Enter your email address and you'll be added right away!

PUBLISHED BY TREESHAKER BOOKS
please visit:
http://www.authorchristopherdschmitz.com

For my KIDS...

Just in case I never told you, there really *were* MONSTERS in your closets.

the Shadowless: The Dark Veil Opens

the Shadowless: The Dark Veil Opens

THE SHADOWLESS

#0

THE DARK VEIL OPENS

1.

Dr. Swaggart, stared at the light. Sterile and fluorescent, it drowned out everything except the beeping. The electronic tones finally ceased momentarily and Swag's eyes refocused; most people called him Swag by his request. Before him stood the corral of humans who scanned arm-loads of items at Bigmart's self-checkout counters.

Bundles of unnecessary sundries and impulse purchases mounded carts accompanied by food in portion sizes that could feed starving third world families, but of a quality which would poison them if ingested. A disinterested woman with a mole on her face tugged at her Bigmart vest as she leafed through a tabloid.

Standing anxiously in a line now only seven-persons-deep, Swag fidgeted with the package of batteries in his hands. It was the only item he needed to purchase. He glanced to his right. Fifteen empty lanes away sat the only open register staffed by a living person; a sign labeled it *Speedy Checkout: 10 items or less*. The three women in line for it each leaned against carts piled to precarious heights as they pushed aside the hair from their *angled bob* hairdos which framed their faces.

He grimaced once he finally pulled into the queue for a register. There wasn't much he could do except wish for curses upon the *Speedy Checkout* quantity abusers. Swag scowled at the logical inconsistency of his inner thoughts: he didn't believe in curses... in a god, any higher power, or even a baseline morality. Curses didn't make sense. They were an old habit.

Swag finally stepped up to the register when his eyes caught a flash of white. He turned his head and spotted the woman in a lab coat that matched his own. Squinting across the distance, he noticed the ID badge was similar, though he could not make out a name. *She must work on the same campus*, he noted, catching a glance of his own ID; he usually unclipped it in public.

Dr. Jimmy Swaggart, it read.

He loathed that name with every fiber of his being. Above everything else, Swag was an empiricist—in fact Swag barely even put faith in what his own eyes told him, most of the time. He had an undergrad philosophy teacher to thank for that.

Swag's hyper-religious parents had saddled him with the unfortunate moniker, and he did his best to obfuscate his full, legal name whenever possible. A piece of masking tape on the bottom of his badge read, *Please call me Swag.*

The fact that his parents had so blatantly named him after a world famous, or infamous in many circles, televangelist had driven a deep rift between the scientist and his parents. Especially during his collegiate years. They talked now—Mother's Day and Christmas, usually—but that damage was permanent.

After swiping his card, he took one last glance at the attractive blond, and headed towards Bigmart's door. Swag wished he was the kind of guy who struck up random conversations with pretty girls… but he was simply not that guy.

"Science is my mistress," he told the confused greeter at the door. A few moments later, Swag slid into the seat of the dilapidated vehicle. His partner, Dr. Raymond Lems, sat behind its wheel.

"We're good to go," Swag said, and the two drove off towards the city park.

"You really think this will give us some hard data?" Raymond asked.

Swag shrugged and reached into the back seat. He retrieved an EMF meter and a few other types of hand-held scanners he'd rented from a local man and social media personality who claimed to be a paranormal investigator. He began changing out the batteries for the fresh ones.

Raymond grinned, "You don't really buy his story that there are ghosts in the park?"

Swag nodded his head with a sarcastic flourish. "He was pretty convinced… and he's the expert. The guy said he had footage of orbs and everything." He rolled his eyes at the notion.

"True science can't rule that out. It can only know what it knows." Raymond returned the smile. "It can't prove that there are no aliens, no angels or ghosts… no God."

Swag scowled as Raymond needled him. He was one of the few folks who knew how violently Swag reacted to his fiercely evangelical upbringing. Swag shot Raymond a nasty glare.

Raymond held up his hands defensively, but put them back promptly when the vehicle's poor wheel alignment threatened to veer them off course. "Hey, I'm just saying."

Swag checked the equipment one last time and then scanned the hand-scrawled equations drawn within his notepad. He was confident in the theories he'd been working on since his undergrad years; they could test them if they could find a subject, and the existence of a subject was an ironic matter of faith. "Well, whatever we find… it won't be a ghost or a god. It will just be some unknown *entity*. Our last couple observations in the field were good, but we need a way to interact with an entity—a safe containment protocol." If they could get one back to the lab, all the better.

The needle bounced on the EMF reader as they exited the vehicle parked adjacent a public park.

Raymond fidgeted with a jar of clear ooze he carried. The jelly-like substance amplified UV radiation wherever applied; based on their mathematics and previous interactions, the scientists had theorized that the UV spectrum rendered the subjected entity inert.

Swag glanced nervously at the jar. *Do we really dare to capture one of these things?* Drums of warning sounded in the primal part of his mind and an image of apocalyptic visions flitted through his brain. Swag promptly rejected it; though he'd tried to jettison all the baggage from his religious upbringing, he found it frequently colored his worldview if he did not diligently guard against it.

Raymond lugged more equipment after him and they systematically canvased the park. They looked like a pair of confused Star Trek costumers, holding the electromagnetic sensors at arm's length as they wandered closer towards a playground.

Chains creaked as nearby kids pumped their legs on the swing-set. Children laughed and shrieked as they rode slides and chased each other in games of tag.

With his eyes locked on the device, Swag didn't watch them with anything more than his peripheral vision. The EMF needle bounced and then spiked when he pointed it to a cluster of short, bushy pines.

Raymond frowned as he glanced aside at the playground. The trees were right next to the children's grounds. "What is it?" He looked over Swag's shoulder as the other scientist knelt by the trees.

Swag bit his lip. "Dunno. Something…" He crawled near the edge of the shade. The noon sun beat down on his back with its relentless heat. His eyes caught the deep black darkness in a hole near the tree's gnarled root. The deep black momentarily fascinated him, demanding the whole of his attention.

Something about darkness had long been able to enchant and equally terrified him. Swag felt the primal draw as the pool of black mesmerized him. Drums pounded in the dark, as if signaling cannibals from the depths of the jungle.

Swag shook away the reverie. The sound was only in his mind and he knew it. Swag reminded himself that it was simply tinitus… blood pumping near his eardrum, *you learned that as a kid… stupid primal-fear caveman brain has been faking me out for three decades now…*

He calmed his pulse by regulating his breathing and rejected the notion that his fear of the dark may have gotten worse since childhood. Swag found denial more comforting than truth.

With the EMF reader, he continued zeroing in on the strongest signal. Something inside the lightless hole emitted a reading.

"What do you think… a rabbit hole?" Raymond asked.

Swag quirked his lips. "No idea." He flashed the tunnel with his light. "It doesn't go very deep."

"Perfect." Raymond emptied the contents of his jar into the hole and then aimed a portable UV lamp at it. "Let's collect this specimen and get it back to the lab."

2.

Swag and Raymond stopped working while their boss entered the site on campus.

Doctor Chandler Howard's eyebrows arched as he scanned the findings. "You're sure these aren't false readings?" he asked. "I see you were using EMF sensors. That and other equipment can sometimes give readings that are highly… suspicious."

The old man was the head of the physics department at the university where they worked. Howard didn't say as much, but all three of the men knew that "ghost hunting" equipment was notorious for generating vague readings that typically allowed paranormal investigators to find evidence they were looking for. As tools, they nearly always validated their users' preconceptions.

Raymond nodded, pushing past their brief foray into the park. "We're pretty confident in our findings," he said, beaming. They'd been working nonstop for the last several days.

"Data is still very early… but the fact that we're gathering data at all is very promising." Swag nodded towards their setup in the lab where pieces of equipment were arranged to grant them easy access. Several UV lamps pointed towards a jar of viscous fluid. Nearby, white boards stood filled with complex computations and a coffee pot emitted the telltale aroma of burned robusta. "After all, until last week this was all theoretical—but now it's practical."

Doctor Howard nodded slowly as he pressed his thin lips into a thin line and scanned the notes again. "This is all very promising stuff. You haven't told anyone about it yet, have you?"

Both men shook their heads.

"Good. Keep it that way. I don't want our university to become a laughingstock of the physics community."

Swag blinked with confusion and a little hurt. "But I thought you just said…"

"I said *to keep it quiet*. I didn't say your research was wrong or faulty in any way." He set the folder down and took a more grandfatherly tone. "Your work has breached a barrier, Doctor Swaggart."

Only Doctor Howard was allowed to call him by his surname. The old professor continued. "Your findings quite possibly connect what many people call *the supernatural* to the realm of the *natural*. I know you've been working on this since before you got your PhD in Quantum Physics, but I don't think your peers will be ready to accept these findings…

not until you have something more solid… and I mean iron clad.”

Raymond nodded, even though Swag scowled. “But we should keep working on it?”

Doctor Howard nodded. “Absolutely. This could be Nobel-level stuff. It could blow the doors wide open with new applications in String Theory and other areas of quantum mechanics.” Something made a clacking noise in the hallway behind them. The professor stroked his chin. “I’m assigning another member to your team,” Doctor Howard said. “Another brilliant young mind who specifically asked to work on the project after reading about some of your older theories printed in some pretty obscure sources.”

“I don’t think we need anyone else on our project,” Swag said. “Raymond and I are more than capable on our own.”

Doctor Howard raised a bushy eyebrow. “You are an intelligent man, Doctor Swaggart. Are you more afraid of dissenting ideas in your think-tank or of having to share the credit when your inevitable breakthrough comes?”

Swag chewed on his lip for a moment and then answered honestly. “Yes.”

Doctor Howard bobbed his head. "Listen, Swag. You've been in my office and seen how big a mess it is, right?"

Swag nodded along dutifully while Raymond crossed his arms and observed.

The old scientist continued, "You know my infamous rack of keys?"

"Next to your diplomas and the old family picture?"

"That's the one. I used to wind up coming home late at night so tired that I'd taken the wrong keys, forcing me to sleep in my car. Until someone got me a rack to organize my keys. Sometimes we all need an outside perspective to help us see through our own mess: one that adds clarity… or in my case, organization, hooks to hang my keys on it and keep my thoughts clear. We all have our weak spots or patterns that it takes an outside source to identify or break… like my wrong-key impulse."

"What keys did you take?" Raymond asked.

Doctor Howard waved off the question. "My old man's house; it's just a couple blocks from here. Place is like a time capsule from nineteen sixty eight." He stood straight as if to differentiate himself from "friend mode" and put himself into "boss mode." He called out, "Please come in, Miss Hiddleston."

The door opened and a perky blond in black heels entered. "Please, call me Jessica," she introduced herself.

"Speaking of weak spots," Raymond mumbled quietly as he sucked in his breath and the pooch of his belly.

Swag recognized her instantly. She was the woman he'd spotted at Bigmart a few days ago.

Doctor Howard grinned at the boys' eagerness to welcome her to their fold. "Miss Hiddleston is a semester away from her final degree and just needs some lab hours to gain her doctorate; I'm sure you'll find her both capable and competent. Let me get out of your way and you can bring her up to speed on your work."

Neither seemed to hear him go as they began talking. Doctor Howard closed the door behind him with a smile.

3.

Jessica stood next to Raymond and Swag. She'd changed over to sensible shoes after the first day on the job—it was easy to see that her first impression had gone over well and she no longer needed the extra effort.

A shipment of lab rats had arrived and her two male counterparts were eagerly devising experiments involving live creatures and their test specimen.

"You guys really think this… this…"

Raymond interrupted her, "Entity?"

She nodded. "You think the *entity* is a kind of life form?"

Swag nodded and scanned the enclosures where the rats were held. "I do. However, it's unlike anything from our reality. We might have to suspend our regular points of reference when dealing with it as a 'life form.'"

"And you think it's from beyond our reality? Are you thinking parallel universes or a multiverse?"

He shook his head. "More like something *alongside* our reality. Not a separate reality, but

15

something that has always coexisted with and intersected with our own."

"So, another dimension of reality?"

Swag neither confirmed nor denied. Her question was too vague. "Imagine you have had anosmia since birth. Anosmia is a condition where you have no sense of smell. It's rare but it can be caused by allergies. If you went your whole life while never experiencing odors but a new allergy medication canceled the anosmia, a whole new sense could suddenly open up that never existed before; how would you react?"

A light flashed in Jessica's eyes as the dots connected in her mind. "You think that the things some people call *supernatural* or *paranormal* have actual connections in this other dimension?"

Swag shrugged. "Yes and no. A lot of that is mumbo jumbo, but sometimes miracles are documented. There are some things that remain unexplained by science. If everyone had anosmia but some people got occasional whiffs of smell, we'd label those experiencing odors as crazy."

Jessica twisted her mouth. "You want to prove miracles?"

Swag continued checking over the equipment.

Raymond shook his head. "The opposite, in fact."

"How would proving miracles happen do the opposite?"

Swag remained apathetic. "If there are empirical, rational *causes* to 'miracles,' we might be able to improve the world without trying to appease flying spaghetti monsters. Reason leads to rationalism," he said pointedly.

"You want to disprove God?" Jessica's voice bordered on offense.

Swag's face softened. "I have a different take on it. I think that, armed with the truth, we have a better chance to advance our species and the welfare of all. Ministers might not like it, but science shouldn't rely on traditions and faith—it must be empirical. I'd rather have an alternate viewpoint from the masses, so long as it's the most accurate one." He scanned Jessica. "Are you open-minded enough to entertain the idea that the things you've grown up thinking and believing might be partially or totally wrong?"

Jessica mulled it over for a moment. "I think so… yes."

They all turned and stared at the illuminated jar that contained the specimen. Swag clapped his hands together. "Excellent! Let's get to work."

The boys excitedly worked their way through most of their processes with Jessica. Recapping what they had already done helped them brainstorm new thoughts and experiments. Their most recent test determined what their sensor readings looked like when the specimen was put into a stasis under UV radiation versus when the entity was in darkness, in its free state.

UV, including sunlight, had a kind of *flattening* effect on it like some kind of restraint.

For her part, Jessica was mostly up to speed on their work already, between updates from Doctor Howard and because she'd read everything that either of them had published. Jessica had been an incoming freshman when Swag and Raymond had worked on their doctoral theses.

Her effervescent personality made it seem like she hung on every word either of them spoke. Raymond and Swag kept glancing towards their new coworker and looking away quickly, both realizing the other male had been leering and hoped the other didn't realize.

Most of the way through the day, Jessica had called for a pizza. She let the other two demolish the remaining slices while she bonded with the lab rats, talking softly to them as if they were intelligent creatures. Like all women, she could feel whenever guys watched her.

Three slices remained. Swag tossed half a crust back into the pizza box and left the room for a moment, headed in the direction of the men's room.

Jessica glanced at the clock and knew they'd be ending the workday any moment. She started cleaning off the table, but Raymond stopped her.

"Just leave the mess where it is," he said.

"I want to pull my weight around here," she insisted.

"No really, let the trash lie."

"It doesn't hurt if I just…"

Swag had returned and hovered in the doorway, holding a cold root beer from the vending machine. "Actually, *it could*, Old Man Jonah has been afraid for his job for a couple years, now. If he's got too little to do, the University might take the opportunity to trim the budget."

She asked, "Trim the budget?"

Raymond made a knife cutting motion across his throat. "They'll fire him."

"It's like shopping carts," Swag said, setting the unopened soda on the table.

Jessica raised an eyebrow.

"Here we go," Raymond sighed.

Swag climbed his imaginary soapbox. "Let me ask you a question. When you go shopping, do you return your shopping cart to the cart coral or abandon it in the parking lot?"

Jessica scoffed, "Just leave it there like some kind of monster? I put it back. People that can't return their carts are the worst…"

"Yeah I've seen the clever, philosophical memes, but you should stop doing that," Swag said emphatically.

Jessica looked surprised.

Swag explained, "Big companies don't hire extra people just so they can help the local economy; that's not why they exist. Hiring extra, unskilled laborers and keeping them on their payroll is a mandatory cost that must have some economic return in order to remain on the books. Sure, I'll return my cart if it's very close to do so—but mainly so I can leave my parking space safely. If there are no carts to return, Bigmart won't hire a person to return them… or worse, they could even decrease staff."

Jessica blinked with disbelief. "They wouldn't do that." She didn't sound so sure.

"How often do you see a waiting line at the *self-checkout registers*?"

She stared blankly for a moment. Swag smiled, knowing he'd convinced her.

"Big business has been training our expectations for years. I remember decades ago most registers were staffed and lines were rare. High school kids even bagged purchases. *Then we self-bagged*; after that, most registers closed and only two or three were ever open. Now it's only one lane open, two if you're lucky, and most folks have been trained to check out on their own. How many people are employed as cashiers now versus five years ago?"

Jessica nodded measuredly, and the door at the back swung open. A black man, perhaps in his early fifties, pushed a cleaning cart into the room. His snowy hair contrasted the sheen on his cheekbones and he smiled broadly at them. "Oh, hello, boys. Who's this?"

"Jessica Hiddleston, this is Jonah Gautreaux," Raymond stated.

"Charmed to meet you," Jonah said with a happy lilt to his voice. He winked at her affably.

Jessica blushed.

Swag raised the soda can and set it by the pizza box. "They had your brand," he said. "And there's a few slices left here for you. They're almost warm even, so I'd get to em quick."

"Thank you kindly, boys," he said, and then got to work, tipping an imaginary hat to Jessica as they left the lab for the evening.

She kept her face neutral, but it was clear she'd seen something different today. Jessica expected that might become a new normal for her.

Swag sighed as they headed towards the community parking lot as a group. Finally, he said, "Sorry if I came off strong… crass… just because I'm an atheist, it doesn't mean I'm some kind of unfeeling monster—shopping carts aside."

Jessica's eyes brightened and she walked towards the bus stop. "Don't sweat it. I'll see you guys tomorrow." She waved at them while walking backwards.

Neither of the guys wanted to tear their eyes away from the pretty blond.

"Tomorrow it is," Raymond said excitedly.

Swag followed him up, "And in a couple weeks, we may even be ready for a live animal experiment."

4.

Behind the science team, the names of different lab rats and their biometric baselines were scrawled upon a whiteboard. Animal trials were about to begin.

"It's so we can be sure we're able to extract the entity from a host," Swag said as he put the dry erase marker down and held aloft the device he'd created.

Jessica stared at it inquisitively. The rats scampered in their glass enclosure nearby.

"What, no rodent exorcist?" Raymond joked.

Swag rolled his eyes. His friend continued, "It looks like an old school garage door opener."

"It's a 'Being Capture Device, Mark I.'" Swag said. "Still just the prototype. I've got some additional things I'd like it to do beyond emitting a QZE field."

Raymond quirked his lips. "Catchy. Maybe we come up with something a little more clever further down the line. BCDM 1 sounds a little too much like an STD you might get from wearing studded leather."

Swag knew Raymond tended to crack jokes when tension was highest—and they had no idea what could happen when they introduced the entity to a rat.

Raymond mumbled, "But it's a good preparatory measure."

Swag nodded and explained the science, Zenotian Para-Existential Fields, and his original theories on both arresting the Quantum Zeno Effect and intensifying it to create a paradoxical field. "Distilled down, the QZE, or Turing Paradox, is the phenomenon of a system's inability to change or evolve while it is being measured or watched." Swag believed his modified QZE fields would antagonize their entity enough to reclaim it for later use without harming the rat.

"Like putting the devil in a headlock?" Jessica joked, taking a cue from Raymond.

Swag shook his head and mumbled, "Eh tu, Jessica?"

She grinned and retrieved the small vial they kept under constant UV light. They'd spent a few days dividing down the contents of the solution and scanning it to confirm the location of their precious subject. They reduced the load down to a half test tube. With a computer model they'd created, scans of the test tube showed the entity in its shuddering, flattened state, like a paramecium being pinched by UV radiation but impotent to free itself.

"Are we ready for this?" Swag asked. Nervous energy rippled through his belly.

His colleagues nodded resolutely and Jessica brought the subject vial over to the enclosure, using tongs to carry it. So far, their theory assumed the entity could travel through solid states like glass or even metal so long as there was no UV radiation to inhibit the entity's movement; due to its extra-dimensional nature, it was unbound by many of the laws of physical reality under many conditions.

Four lab rats scampered through the cedar shavings as Jessica loaded the opened tube into the steel water dispenser for the rats. The entire vial fit through a flip-top lid and slipped into the darkness.

Raymond wheeled a sensor towards the cage and pointed it towards the water bottle. "It's definitely in there. Scans show the entity is active, no longer repressed by UV."

Swag stroked his chin and watched the critters run around within the cage. Jessica and Raymond joined him with clipboards in hand as they prepared to record any changes.

One of the rats hopped up to the dispenser and took a sip, nibbling against the ball-block that held the water inside the reservoir. The rat stopped and then turned to stare at the humans with a new kind if intrigue.

Raymond checked the sensor and frowned. He spoke breathily, "The entity is no longer in the bottle." He adjusted the sensor array and pointed it at the rat. "There you are, you little devil," he grinned. "The entity is definitely inside the rat."

Swag grinned; part one of their experiment was a success and they'd hoped to test a second theory. He took a UV light and shone it directly at the rodent. It cocked its head. "Any change?"

Raymond shook his head. "The entity is *not* affected by UV light while inside a host... no flattening phenomenon."

The scientists stared at the rodent for several minutes. Presence of the entity appeared to have no effect on the rodent, aside from giving the rat a sense of higher reasoning. As much as they studied the creature, it seemed to also be *studying them.*

"Unnerving," Raymond said as the rodent continued watching him with its beady eyes. The other rats scampered back and forth along the back wall of the enclosure, suddenly keeping their distance from their furry peer. "But not dangerous."

Jessica fidgeted with her pen as she watched and waited for any observations to record. The stylus slipped out of her fingers and tumbled to the floor. She leaned down to pick it up and drew the eyes of both male scientists as she bent at the waist.

No sooner had they succumbed to the distraction than the rat sprang into action. It leapt upon the other rodents in the enclosure almost like it was having a seizure, except far more malevolent. It snarled with almost canine fervor while its furry victims shrieked with helpless squeals.

The science team stood straight and watched in terror as the table supporting the glass-walled enclosure shook. Blood and viscera scattered across the wood shavings. Sickly sounds replaced the high-pitched panic sounds.

Shuddering with pure hate and rage, the rodent that had consumed the entity stared at the human trio with its beady eyes. The puddle of gore it left in its wake was no longer recognizable.

Raymond broke the silence. "'Little Devil' is right," he muttered. "Is… is that thing possessed?"

Swag grimaced. "That's a religious term. It's nonsense under these conditions and I don't like the connotation it could bring up… *afflicted*," he offered. "I think that might be a more fitting term."

Raymond shot him an askew look. "Well I'm still nicknaming this thing Little Satan," he said as he returned his attention to the cage. The rat stared at him, white pelt coated in congealing blood.

No sooner did he look the rodent in the eye than it attacked. It flung itself at the glass barrier with supernatural strength and agility, shattering the container walls.

Jessica screamed.

Swag howled, "The door! The door! Close it—we can't let this thing escape!"

The rat plopped down onto the linoleum tile in a splatter of red which trailed off momentarily as Little Satan skittered across the floor with unnerving speed.

Raymond reached the door first and slammed it shut.

Little Satan shrieked like some kind of demon-fiend in a mid-October Hollywood blockbuster and then charged the scientist.

Reacting on pure instinct, Raymond punted the rat across the room with a startled yelp. The rodent smacked against the wall with surprising force and bounced to the ground. Against the odds, it hopped back to its feet again and hissed, more ferociously than before, and then it sprinted to attack Raymond.

This time Raymond covered his face with his arms and yelled.

Swag intercepted it just in time and pressed the button on his BCDM 1. The rodent staggered to a halt as if the sustained physical damage finally caught up to it and the rat wretched the contents of its stomach onto the tile. It seemed suddenly harmless, like any other lab rat.

"The sensor!" Swag snapped his fingers and Jessica hurried to wheel it over.

With his fingers still on the Mark 1's activation button, the rat tried to stagger away. It got barely a meter away when Swag stomped on it with one swift, violent motion. He hooked a finger in the heel of his shoe and then peeled it off as quickly as he could. Falling to his rump, he tossed his sock away, too. They didn't yet know what they were dealing with and how the entity could move.

"We got it!" Raymond yelped excitedly,

Swag looked at him and Jessica. The laser-sensor array was pointed at the small puddle of rat vomit. "You're sure?"

Raymond nodded. Only then did Swag release his finger on the Mark 1.

Still on his butt, Swag swallowed hard and then began laughing like a madman.

Jessica raised an eyebrow. Her cheeks were flush with blood and endorphins. She smirked with a chuckle.

"It's not all that funny, you guys," Raymond said. "Little Satan just tried to kill me."

"But think of all the data we got from that encounter," Swag said. "But we should probably order a new habitat made from bullet proof glass."

Jessica wrote that down.

"And some new rats." Swag stared at the puddle of sick. "Now we just have to harvest the entity again."

"I thought fancy garage door opener was a 'Capture Device?'" Raymond said.

"I also called it a work in progress," Swag merely shrugged as he retrieved the equipment to collect the entity. He mumbled, "Can you imagine what might happen if one of these things, these… entities, got into a person?"

Christopher D. Schmitz

5.

Raymond heard a knock on his door. He was drop-dead tired. All the endorphins from the earlier excitement had worn off and he felt totally drained, like a hollow shell.

He shuffled towards the door to his apartment and a zombie-puppet scene from Jim Henson's *Dark Crystal* floated through his mind. Raymond felt very much like a poor gelfling drained of his essence by the skeksis. He turned the knob and opened his door.

Swag stood there, holding a pink box. "Surprise," he said, pushing his way inside. He set the box down and pulled out his mobile to fire off a quick text.

"This isn't how surprise parties work," Raymond noted, walking to check the box. His spirits lifted somewhat at the arrival of a familiar face.

The box had many price reduction stickers on it from the store. Raymond flipped the lid to find what had obviously started its life as a wedding cake but had been refrosted with an animated Disney character to reskin it for a child's birthday party. "Cake?"

Another knock at the door. Swag opened it to reveal Jessica. She lugged in a full case of beer and set it on the table.

"Of course, cake," Swag chuckled. "Today was important. We made a huge discovery… I've been talking about these theories for years, Raymond. Today we leapt off the ledge. We gotta celebrate it—today was our Kitty Hawk."

Jessica cracked a beer. "There's never a bad reason for cake. Heck, my uncle bought a wedding cake with only a groom on it and threw a bachelor party to celebrate his divorce. And this… this cake…"

The three of them stared into the box together. Jessica made air quotes to indicate *"cake."*

"God, that thing is ugly," Swag admitted, staring at the confectionary horror.

Whoever had tried to doctor it up had scraped off the nuptial accoutrements and tried to add a crude *Finding Nemo* fish. The new frosting job looked like a kindergartner had freehanded it.

Swag shrugged, accepted a beer from their lab assistant, and explained, "A five dollar cake is still a cake."

They each took an over-sized slice and laughed off Raymond's near-death experience and tried to eat their piece. It had gone stale days ago and required copious amounts of beer to wash it down.

After a few beers each, and an aborted attempt to finish her slice, Jessica looked at the wedding cake and laughed. "Ya know, I was a little confused at first," she admitted to Swag. "I figured you two lived together."

Raymond raised his brows. "I know we spend a lot of time together, but… we're separate people."

Swag cocked his head. "I'm not sure what you mean." His words had just begun to take on a slight slur.

She shrugged. "I guess there's a general kind of vibe with you guys. People on campus generally figure you guys are a gay couple."

The two scientists looked at each other askance. "Um… no," said Swag.

"Hey," Raymond defended. "I could make some guy very happy, thank you very much… But no," he said to Jessica. "Definitely not gay."

"And neither of you have ever been married?"

Both of them watched her. She had to have felt their interest, unless she was as clueless about matters of the heart as Raymond and Swag had proved themselves over the years.

"Never," Swag said.

Raymond shook his head. "The right girl has never come along," he said, glossy eyed.

Swag's eyes flitted to Raymond and then back to Jessica. Despite the drunk buzz, he could feel the looming tension. If it had been a footrace, he would have felt Raymond pulling into the lead. "But things are starting to look optimistic," he said.

This time, Raymond shot Swag a look. "Things look good, indeed."

Jessica gave them both a weird look and laughed. Obviously a girl who could hold her weight, she passed them each another beer and pushed her cake away. "I think this cake is a lost cause, boys, but I'm betting we can kill off the rest of these beers."

They clinked their drinks together and threw them back.

6.

A radio blasted in the back of the lab, tuned to the local college station. Swag, Raymond, and Jessica interconnected a series of sensors and other equipment for the next round of observations. Jessica seemed to sway to the music with a certain grace as the station cycled through a few classics. Both the males glanced at her appreciatively and tapped their toes to Jimi Hendrix. She'd improved the ambiance of their lab, in addition to proving herself a capable and competent researcher.

The song switched and a familiar melody played, swelling to the chorus and all three belted out in unison, "Sweet Caroline!"

With twinkling eyes, Jessica shuffled backwards and danced a little to the tune. "Alright, guys," she said, "Who's gonna dance with me."

They both grinned, but neither volunteered.

"Come on, Swag?"

He shook his head.

"Raymond?"

Raymond shook his head. "No thanks. Not a dancer."

"What do you mean?" Swag argued. "I thought they called you Sugar Ray Ray when you were a teenager? Your mother made you take tap dance lessons through middle school."

Raymond glared daggers at him, but stiffened his neck and locked eyes on Swag as he stepped in to dance with Jessica. Finally, he laughed, forgetting that his friend had pushed him into it. Raymond smiled and shook his legs goofily with Jessica.

Swag's neck went flush as he watched them together. The song finally ended and Jessica and Raymond chuckled, further irking Swag with a mild fit of jealousy. "Well, some of us were on the football team and didn't have time for dancing."

"You weren't on the football team," Raymond fired back. "You told me about it when we were freshmen in college. You took stats."

"I was still a vital part of the team," Swag insisted, pride wounded. His mother had thought the sport too violent and wouldn't let him actually participate.

Jessica grimaced, uncomfortable at the friends quarreling. She went back to her work in silence. Behind her, Swag and Raymond kept tossing petty barbs at each other, completely forgetting the project, despite a fairly tight time table. They had hoped to borrow some lab equipment tomorrow from another department. They needed their station prepped and ready for its arrival in the morning.

The other two finally resumed working, each on either side of Jessica, but continued to mumble insults and passive aggressive curses at each other as though the other party could not hear it. Having known been the other person's confidant for many years, they each had ample ammunition.

"It's no wonder your mother…" Swag's voice mumbled into something incoherent.

Jessica's cheeks reddened.

Raymond spat one back. "At least my mother wasn't a phony nutbag who ended up…"

Jessica stood straight up with eyes wide open. "Sorry, boys. Something is going on here," she backed away with her hands held up as if trying to flee a gunman. "Right now, I just *can't even…* whatever is bugging you guys, figure it out."

She left.

Swag and Raymond glared daggers at each other as she departed. Both their necks had reddened with shame. Raymond bit his cheek and

Swag refused to meet Raymond's gaze. They worked the rest of the afternoon in silence.

7.

A storm brewed on the horizon as Swag left the lab and he could feel a static charge in the air as he walked the long way around the campus in order to avoid his partner. His stomach soured and grumbled to match the distant rumble of a thunderhead. He wasn't hungry as much as stressed.

"Stupid Raymond," he muttered beneath his breath. "It was obvious he could tell I was kind of into her." His mother's voice rattled around in his mind. *King Solomon said to split the child in two.*

He squinched his lips together and silently cursed. Another roll of thunder. *Of all the times to walk and clear my head, it's gotta be when it suddenly rains? How cliche.*

His mother invaded again. *Elijah told King Ahab to gather food and drink because, even after all that time without it, he heard the rain coming.*

Swag grumbled and heard the distant hiss of droplets falling. He ducked into the nearest building. A pub sat on the opposite side of the street; it was a squat, ugly little building that some of the local professors were known to frequent. He ambled over towards the bar and took a seat at a barstool.

He looked up towards the tiny box-set television mounted on the wall where the news program played. An inset weather warning flashed in the lower corner of the picture. He tried to get a better look at the red and green weather pattern when a burly bartender blocked his view.

The man set a napkin on the table in lieu of a coaster. "What'll it be?"

Swag nearly dismissed him. He rarely drank, as evidenced by the fact he barely remembered beers the other night with Jessica and Raymond. *Stupid Raymond,* he stewed. "Bourbon," Swag said, trying to sound like he did this all the time.

Not a fool, the bartender smirked. He set a tumbler on the napkin and poured the scientist a drink from a bottle on the lowest shelf, leaving Swag to wallow in his misery and watch the television.

The weather picture looked like a flash storm. It would pass in an hour or so. Luckily, the television program might prove interesting.

Swag took a sip of the glass and did his best not to wince. He glanced apprehensively at the smirking bartender who'd given him the swill and then looked back to the screen where a ticker asked, *The next Waco?* and identified the speaker on camera, a slightly pudgy, angry man with a goatee and shaved head, as "'Reverend' Jethro Diggleton.'"

The screen switched to scenes of a younger and trimmer Diggleton beating on people in rings that looked like cast-offs from some backyard wrestling circuit. They didn't look like fair fights and Diggleton's opponents looked out of shape, untrained, or ill prepared.

Swag struggled to keep up with the subtitles and there was no audio on the box-set. He took another swig from his glass and stopped caring about the program. Swag returned to the source of his recent frustration. *Raymond.*

The adjacent barstool's feet squawked and a new resident took ownership. Doctor Howard's elbow grazed Swag's. Their eyes met and Swag recognized the much older scientist; there was a pained look in the depths of his eyes and the man seemed to nurse a hurt far deeper than Swag was feeling.

Without a word the bartender placed Doctor Howard's glass and poured him a double shot of Bulleit.

Doctor Howard spoke first, "You look like a man with trouble on your mind, Doctor Swaggart." His voice sounded strained.

Swag nodded. He was certain that the man who had all but been his mentor was about to serve up some morsel of wisdom as if he'd cut it off an apple with a pocket knife.

Doctor Howard sighed. "That makes two of us." He glanced at the television where they showed Diggleton losing badly to opponents when he was more equally matched. The screen switched to shots of him at the gun range shooting targets. The caption ticker recorded "the fighting preacher's" words. *...our time is coming. You don't understand. None of you understand, and that's why you won't survive what's coming: an apocalypse, a shaking unlike anything you've ever felt! America is filled with sheep! And you know scripture says that at the end times the "wolf will lie down with the lamb—"* He pulled up his sleeve to reveal a wolf tattoo on his arm. The ticker completed, *—Wolves never go hungry...*

"Lots of troubles in the world," Doctor Howard drained his glass and tapped its rim twice. He nodded towards the television. "Idiots with a platform only making things worse." The bartender promptly refilled him and Doctor Howard turned to face him. "What's on your mind, son?"

Swag took another sip of liquid courage and told him as much of his story as he could without making himself look like an idiot. Even that version still made him sound petty and jealous once he'd spoke it aloud. "I feel kind of stupid, now."

Doctor Howard shrugged. "We do stupid things whenever love is concerned." He sipped again. "Of course, you don't know if you love her… and you don't know Raymond's real intentions, and neither has even asked the girl how she feels, right?"

Swag blushed and he stared into his glass. He nodded to acknowledge the facts.

Sipping again, Doctor Howard said, "Love is a wild ride… way more potent than that stuff they're making across the campus for that new pharmaceutical trial… it's practically meth, that stuff." He rotated his tumbler in between his hands so that the wedding ring on his finger clinked against the glass. "It should be celebrated… love, I mean—not drugs. Love is why we have anniversaries… yesterday would have been mine." He lifted his glass in salute and whispered the name of his beloved, "Joanie."

Swag knew Joanie had passed away a couple years ago.

Doctor Howard exhaled long and hot. "One thing I know: unless you really like it that way, it's not good to be alone."

"I thought you had a son? I've seen photos on your desk," Swag said, wondering why Doctor Howard wasn't with him for what seemed like a difficult anniversary.

Doctor Howard looked into his tumbler for a long moment as if searching for the right answer. Deep crimson glowed at the edges of his eyelids, as if they hurt to blink. "Yeah," he said, and threw back the rest of the drink. "I did."

The bartender meandered back towards the liquor shelf again in search of the old professor's preferred drink.

Something in the way Doctor Howard said it clued Swag in. He did not ask further questions about his son.

The bartender turned to look at Swag and his drink. He waggled the bottle. "Top you off?"

Swag shook his head. He still had half a glass left and the rain had finally stopped. The professor remained fixed to his seat and Swag thought back to his problem. He'd heard the line before: *It is not good that a man should be alone.* His mother quoted it often, along with many other bible verses… despite Swag's position, he knew there was at least some truth to that one.

That same rule could apply to friendships, I suppose. He knew how to handle the situation with Raymond. Swag glanced at Doctor Howard and decided not to abandon him. *It's not good for a man to be alone…*

"Actually, yeah," Swag called to the bartender. "Top me off." He could sit a while with the old man.

8.

Raymond answered the knocking at his door. It swung open to reveal his partner, Swag. "What do you want?" Raymond groused.

Swag held up a half gallon of chocolate milk. "I can't rightfully drink without my drinking buddy," he said, pushing his way inside.

Raymond wrinkled his nose at the cloy scent of bourbon that still clung to Swag. "You smell like my grandpa's den… and you *hate* chocolate milk."

"I know," replied Swag as he poured two tall glasses of brown milk. "But you love it." He pulled the nasty cake out of the fridge, knowing his former college roommate never threw away food, even bad food, until it was well beyond eating.

Raymond cocked an eyebrow.

Swag took a sip of chocolate milk and grimaced. "God, that's awful."

"What do you want?" Raymond injected a threatening tone into his voice.

"To apologize. Listen," Swag slid a crusty piece of cake towards his friend. "I'm sorry about earlier… I think I got kind of hot headed when I saw you with Jessica."

Raymond flattened his lips and took a seat, draining half of his chocolaty glass. "Yeah. I could tell. You really like her?"

Swag shrugged. "Maybe? I don't know. I like her… I think there's a certain kind of spark there, and we certainly have some things in common."

Raymond bobbed his head, though he frowned. "I know what you mean. I feel the same way about her." He fingered the plate with the 'cake.' "What do you propose?"

Swag shrugged. "Well, I think it's stupid to risk losing my best friend over a girl—even if she is pretty awesome."

"I feel the same way. Maybe we make a pact?"

Swag shot him an interested look.

Raymond continued. "Neither of us dates her? Jessica is off-limits. From now on, she's just one of the guys."

Swag nodded and agreed. It was the most logical course and it was the only one that didn't put Jessica on the spot. After all, she hadn't technically expressed any direct interest in *either* of them, anyway. Nobody lost face and they could go back to business as usual.

"Sorry I brought up the tap dancing," Swag said. "That was a low blow."

Raymond shrugged it off. It hadn't earned him any social disgrace in years and it rarely bothered him anymore; he hadn't expected it to resurface from so close a source. "Heck, I'll come in and tap dance for you and Jessica both if you'll tell me the real reason you moved out of our apartment two years ago."

Jessica had been right about their living arrangement. At least once upon a time, anyway.

Swag shook his head and pulled his cake apart with a fork. *It shouldn't call itself that,* Swag thought, deflecting from even his innermost thoughts. *This cake is a lie...* and he didn't want to make up another one to keep his secrets from his closest. "Sorry. Like I said before..."

"It's private?"

Swag nodded. Science was his life—his mind was his greatest asset and he saw his power to observe the empirical as his greatest tool… he could not tell even his best friend about the voices in his mind, the fell whispers and drums he heard whenever he stared into the dark. A theoretical physicist who had to sleep with the lights on? Nobody would trust such a person's research.

"Alright then, keep your secrets. But I'm here, man."

Swag nodded again.

Sipping on his glass, Raymond took a bite of cake. "It's not too bad if you moisten it up some with the milk." he said.

Swag took a huge swig of chocolate milk and dug his fork into the cake. Both things revolted him and he hoped they'd cancel each other out.

They didn't.

But for the sake of his friend, he could pretend that it was fine.

Raymond paused mid-chew; he stared dumbly at the hunk of 'cake.' "Breakthrough… I wonder if UV light acts as a binding agent on the entity… like how the milk locks down these nasty crumbs and helps wash them down."

Swag shrugged. "We already assumed as much."

"No… I mean in relation to the para-existential field."

Swag locked eyes with. "You mean that while the entity isn't bound by our dimension's physics, it is while under a binding agent that is subject to UV radiation… like the analog gel or a host: like the rat?"

Raymond nodded enthusiastically and grinned—the cake was becoming more important by the minute.

If he was right, certain agents like UV *could bind* Little Satan to the physical world's rules while locked inside a "host." They could enact a whole series of tests, if so… at least experiments that would be relevant to one of the entity's modes while in a hosted-state. Swag checked his timepiece, "Let's head back to the lab and set up for a few additional tests to confirm that theory tomorrow."

There was no mistaking the eagerness in his voice. The boys were back in business—and tomorrow they would put Little Satan at their mercy.

9.

An old tune pumped through the custodian's headphones. *Old white boy music,* his father had called it. Jonah Gautreaux didn't care; he still loved Johnny Cash… sometimes he was in an Elvis mood, even.

Jonah whistled along as the mp3 player in his hip pocket pushed his classic tunes via his wired headphones. He brushed the curling lines of cable aside and pushed his mop bucket and cleaning cart into his favorite section of the University.

A broad grin spread across his face when he spotted the soda can waiting on the lab bench, as was normal for any given Wednesday. Even though Dr. Swag had left him something special regularly for over a year, now, Jonah never took it for granted.

Beneath the catchy grooves of *Ring of Fire* Jonah mumbled, "Something about that boy… he gets me." He cracked the soda and read Swag's post-it note. *I'm sure they don't pay you what you're worth, but thanks anyway—here's a little something to say thanks.*

He began to mop around the floor as the song changed to Cash's *God's Gonna Cut You Down*. He hummed along and sang the lyrics in a low voice. "…tell that long tongue liar."

Swish, swish. The mop head flicked in and out of the table legs. "Tell that midnight rider…" *Swish, swish.* "Tell the rambler, the gambler, the back biter…" *Swish, swish.*

He spun around with the mop still firmly upon the tiles, loosening dirt and cleaning linoleum. He shifted between humming sounds and lyrics as he grew closer and closer to the staged equipment. Jonah would not take much longer. He was both quick and good at what he did—and that was always a problem with hourly work.

"Workin' in the dark against your fellow man… hmmm, hmmm-uh-hmmm, hmmm. What's done in the dark will be brought to the light."

The frayed edges of his mop caught the locked wheel beneath some kind of laser system on a mobile cabinet mounting system and the handle slipped free from his grip. It swung like a fulcrum and hurled towards the lit glass tube at the center of Swag's research.

Jonah leapt for it—too late. The glass vial smashed and leaked goo all over his hands. "Oh no, oh no, oh no…" Jonah had already tossed his ear buds aside and scrambled for his telephone. He scanned the walls for emergency contact info. He needed to call someone quick to confirm whether the mysterious substance could be harmful to him;

Jonah was no science whiz, and the busted tube looked an awful lot like those nuclear or bio-hazard containers he'd seen in spy movies.

He rummaged through his cart, but could not locate his mobile. Jonah patted his waistband and suddenly remembered that it was in his hip pocket. *Funny I didn't remember that right away,* he thought as he slipped his hands into them.

There was no light inside his pockets.

Jonah only rummaged inside for a split second, and then he began cackling like a madman. Unbound within the darkness, Little Satan had found a new host.

Contorting and twitching like a frenzied animal, the custodian sprinted for the door with the energy of a man half his age and far more athletic than Jonah Gautreaux had been even in his prime. He snarled and kicked the door open, busting it free from frame and hinges.

A bewildered pair of coeds stared at Jonah-who-was-not-Jonah. One looked frightened, the other indignant. He leapt upon them and strangled the first, choking the life out of her. The other student fled as she screamed in terror, running in the direction of the campus security office.

Still holding the lifeless student by the neck, Jonah looked up. His eyes yellowed and shot through with pulsing crimson. The pupils contracted into tiny pinpoints of light. They turned up and met Swag's gaze.

Swag's jaw hung agape. Next to him, Raymond trembled, "J-Jonah?"

"That's not Jonah," Swag said, hedging to the side so he could keep his distance.

Jonah—Little Satan—hissed as he locked eyes on Swag with a predatory gaze, "Do you remember me? All who know me recognize the sound of my voice, little Jimmy Swaggart. You heard me speak as a child. You are one of my fold." His voice was as gnarled and twisted as the wreckage of the door behind him.

Swag's voice dried up when he looked the monster in the eye and he could not muster a response. The dark drums began pounding in his ears, louder than even during the darkest nights alone in his room. Finally he looked to Raymond and managed, "Jonah is afflicted... Little Satan somehow got into him."

A siren split the air across the quad and the afflicted custodian flung the lifeless student's body towards them before fleeing across the campus, shrieking like a banshee as he went. With a sickly tumble, the lifeless body tumbled to an awkward rest at Swag's feet.

The sounds of further death and destruction followed Jonah's trail of terror.

10.

Alternating red and blue lights flashed in the laboratory window. Swag and Raymond had sneaked away before the police arrived. They hid inside the lab, knowing the cops would have no idea how to handle something like this… whatever *this* truly was. The scientists had to confirm their suspicion before the police detained any witnesses—and there was very little likelihood they would believe the scientists' explanation for the murder.

Through the busted laboratory door, all the evidence lay before them. Jonah's cleaning cart and mop bucket remained where they'd been abandoned: only a few feet from the staged setup area where they'd prepped for tomorrow morning's experiments. At the center of it all lay the UV containment tube. Its glass was broken and the analog gel had leaked from the tube and onto the floor.

Raymond held the EMF meter and scanned the room. He shook his head. "Little Satan is definitely not here… it's in Jonah," he confirmed.

Swag was already on the phone talking with Jessica he turned so Raymond could hear him. "What do you mean, 'Jonah's on the news?'"

Raymond looked up and began fumbling with the television remote, activating the screen at the back of the room. A moment later, they had him on the screen.

Jonah was rampaging through town and pursued by local police. The feed was shaky and taken from a distance, most likely a news helicopter. Jonah bled from his chest and shoulder with what looked like bullet holes. The madman trashed storefronts and chased people short distances like a rabid animal; he dodged out of the way from cops as they tried to hem him in, weapons drawn. Jonah's wounds looked grievous, but didn't appear to slow him any.

"Alright," Swag said. "We'll meet you there." He ended the call and dropped his mobile phone into a pocket.

"What are we going to do?" Raymond asked. He suggested, "This could be our fault."

Swag grimaced. "We didn't break the jar—it's not our fault," he insisted, "but we *can* do something. Grab the UV lights; we're going to catch Little Satan."

"Wait... what? He's literally rampaging like Godzilla and bullets aren't even slowing him down."

Swag snatched their spare entity collection tube and double checked the UV feature's batteries to make sure it could hold the entity. He thought back to Bigmart and the checkout lines. *This all started with batteries...* He pressed the button and lights lit on both ends of the forearm length cylinder they would use to hold the fiend and then grabbed a few warning stickers from the lab's supply cabinet.

"Jessica is already there," Swag stated, clipping the Mark 1 device to his pocket. "She happened to be downtown already. Come on. It's only a few blocks."

Raymond muttered a string of curses below his breath and grabbed two handheld UV lights. Moments later, they were speeding downtown in Swag's dilapidated car. When the phone rang he tossed it to Raymond who answered.

"You're where?" Raymond got Jessica's address and shouted it to Swag. The loud noise of a helicopter drowned him out and he had to repeat himself.

"Get out of the way!" Swag howled as people fleeing the area darted in front of his car. Swag was already driving recklessly. Finally, he pulled off and they abandoned the car with the passenger wheels perched halfway over the sidewalk. "It's only a block or two that way," Swag yelled, flinging the door open.

Screams and pops of small arms fire peppered the air. They went around to the back side of the block and sprinted through the empty street, turning up a block later and into an alleyway.

From the passage Jessica waved to them and they regrouped. The two guys panted hard.

"This is—this is crazy," Raymond choked between gulps of air.

Jessica's gaze was serious. "I remember what the rat did… think of the damage a person could do—we have to stop the entity."

Gun shots rang out. They were extremely close, just beyond the mouth of the alleyway.

"What's the plan?" Swag asked.

Jessica gulped. "Do you have all the equipment you need to catch this thing?"

Swag and Raymond nodded nervously. Jessica snatched one of the UV lamps.

"We have no idea if the Mark 1 will work on Jonah like it did on the rat," Raymond said, fumbling with the device. "He could kill us before we can even try it."

"When we first harvested the thing, it was unbound and we isolated it with UV and the analog gel." Swag shook the UV collection container filled with goo.

"Well, figure it out," she spat, turning to leave. "You don't have much time."

Raymond yelped, "Where are you going?"

"To lure it in. Remember the rat's eyes? That burning intelligence?" She jogged further through the alley where it exited in a narrow passage between two brick buildings. "Let's see if it remembers me."

"Intelligent?" Raymond asked. "Do you really think…"

"I don't think we should take chances," Swag said, crouching behind a dumpster. His partner joined him.

Jessica leaned out of the alley and screamed as a police officer nearly backpedaled into her. He fired his tactical shotgun and then turned to flee.

Jonah leapt upon the policeman and grabbed him by the shoulder, swinging the man as if he were a doll. He smashed the officer into the brick work, breaking his neck and nearly tearing the arm free of its torso. The afflicted janitor locked eyes on Jessica who turned and fled deeper into the alley.

Snarling, the beast pursued and gained on her. *He definitely remembered.*

Jessica screamed the whole way. She was only a few steps from the dumpster where the rest of the team hid, and barely a step beyond the afflicted man's reach. Suddenly, her knee buckled and she tumbled forward.

The uncannily fast Jonah tried to snatch her by the hair, but her fall helped her evade his grasp. She tumbled three yards past the dumpster and Swag threw himself out of hiding and engaged the Mark 1 device, pointing it directly at Jonah while at close range.

Jonah, his body riddled with bullet holes and scattershot, staggered to a stop. His eyes seemed to suddenly recognize the scientist. "Sw-Swag? Doctor Swag, I don't... I don't feel so..."

He began to cough and wretch like he might puke and Swag sprang into action, dumping out some of the analog gel and holding the open tube out for the man to puke into. "Lights! The lights!" he screamed.

Jessica and Raymond flicked on their handheld UV beams and shined it on Swag's hands so the entity couldn't unbind from the fluids and slip into Swag. Most of the vomit went into the containment unit. The rest onto Swag's arms.

"I—I don't… what happen…" With a raspy death rattle, Jonah collapsed and exhaled his final breath several feet away. What little blood still remained in him poured from the wounds and puddled in the alley's floor.

They kept the lights on Swag's forearms and knew any amount could be enough for transmission. Swag didn't want to risk exposing the others and so he dropped the Mark 1 and activated the container before setting it down. Jessica kept her light on Swag's extended hands while Raymond checked the cylinder with the EMF reader.

"It's over. We got him," Raymond said, device pointed at the containment tube. "Readings consistent with an entity under UV. Little Satan is bound."

Boots tromped down the alleyway. The police would be on top of them any second. Swag dug into his pocket and withdrew a radioactivity warning sticker and slapped it on the containment unit to make sure the authorities didn't tamper with it. He looked up just in time to see the business end of a dozen firearms pointed in his face.

"Back away!" a voice barked.

Swag complied, joining the others with his hands held high. Together they watched the police clap Jonah's lifeless body into restraints before checking it for vitals. Raymond hissed something into his ear, but he only heard the low thrumming of those ethereal drums pounding in the recess of his mind and the fell whispers that plagued the darkness.

11.

Inside the police station, Swag and Raymond sat on a wooden bench with Jessica in between them. They each had their wrists handcuffed to the other. Amid the chaos, they'd luckily been kept together rather than detained separately. They weren't technically suspects, but their presence at the scene, along with their connection to Jonah, had an inherent suspicion.

When the hall had cleared, Raymond sighed. "They're probably going to see that our laboratory badges are all for the same location... fifty feet from where Jonah killed that first woman."

"That's not so bad," Jessica said. "There's no link there."

"Except that Raymond and I were at the scene when it happened and slipped away before the cops could find any witnesses matching our description, and then we appeared two miles away at the site of all the carnage." He blasted a puff of hot frustration through his nose and let a few tortured seconds pass in silence. "They said he killed seven cops... wounded a bunch of others."

"Okay. Yeah. That's bad," Jessica admitted. Someone was supposed to interrogate them soon. "What are we going to say? Do we have some kind of story?"

Raymond stared at her and blinked. "I was going to go with the truth. It's the only thing we won't corporately bungle. Police interrogators are good at poking holes in lies."

Jessica slumped with dejection clearly written on her face. "They'll never believe the truth."

Swag leaned back and clanked his head against the wall in defeat. "Agreed. But it's the only thing that won't make us look like Jonah's direct accomplices."

"What about indirect links?" Raymond asked. "I know you always left the old man a soda."

Swag shot him a sidelong look and cocked an eyebrow.

"I'm just saying," Raymond insisted, "this thing is all over the news. *Someone* is going to take the fall for this—guilty or not… someone's got to be punished for all of this. And it won't be Jonah."

"You don't think…"

Raymond overrode Swag. "From the horse's mouth, man. Reagan said, 'The nine most terrifying words in the English language are: I'm from the Government, and I'm here to help.'"

They sat a few moments more in silence.

"Here's the plan," Swag said. "When we get our phone calls, Raymond call a lawyer for you and me. Jessica, you should call your own and try to act like we randomly bumped into each other downtown—you've got enough of an alibi for that. Throw us under the bus. You can probably still get away from whatever Raymond and I are about to get caught up in."

"What about you?" she asked Swag.

"I'll call Doctor Howard. Maybe he can confirm what we've been studying." He grimaced and hoped Doctor Howard would be sober. *As if the old professor didn't have enough problems of his own right now.* "I'm pretty sure that we're gonna wind up in prison," Swag sighed, banging his head on the wall again.

Jessica asked, "Any regrets?"

Swag shrugged and looked from her to Raymond. "Just the one."

12.

Aside from a warning not to deactivate the power to Little Satan's containment cell under a fictitious threat of a radiation leak, neither Swag, Jessica, or Raymond had given the police any report except requests for their phone call.

Finally, Professor Howard arrived and took a seat across from Swag. "The police chief is an old poker buddy of mine and I convinced him to give me some private time with you. Nothing is being recorded." He fixed Swag with a firm but empathetic stare, "Jimmy… what the hell happened?"

Swag told him everything. Everything they'd seen and deduced. Everything they suspected the entity could do. How it moved… the rats. "This thing is real… my theories were correct All of them. And what we found is terrifying."

When Swag was done, a long pause stretched between them and Doctor Howard asked, "Do you really think 'the devil made him do it' is a wise defense?"

"Entity," Swag corrected. "Little Satan is just a stupid nickname Raymond gave it."

"Whatever. They media and police are only going to hear 'demonic possession.' It's how their minds work."

"It's not the truth."

Doctor Howard sighed. "This honestly can't get out like that, Swag. The full truth of what happened can't be made plain—people won't understand it. You'll be laughed off the campus. If your work is about to blow the lid off Pandora's Box, then there's more data that we'll need—that the human race might need—if these things are all as dangerous as Jonah's entity, and you can't know that with just the one sample. You can't abort your career so soon. You'd never work again and no scientist would revisit your work for a century."

"I have verifiable facts and hard science."

Doctor Howard looked down his nose at him. "And when they laugh you out of the scientific community for your 'demons in the darkness' theory and do so in the name of 'good science,' who will be the ones armed in the fall out?"

Swag only stared at him. He was unsure what Doctor Howard meant.

"*Me*, Swag. *Us*... the whole university. People aren't ready to accept that this kind of thing—demon, entity, or whatever it is—is really out there… not yet. They'll call your entire education a failure. The university will falter after enrollment drops. Everyone from the chancellor to the custodian will be out of their jobs. We've got to put a lid on this—embargo all of your data, immediately."

Swag swallowed hard.

"Have you told anyone else? Who knows about your research?"

He shook his head. "Only myself, Raymond, and Jessica. We were waiting for advice from you… and the lawyers."

Doctor Howard swore. "The lawyers, right… we'll have to hope they keep it under wraps as privileged information." He rummaged a hand through his hair and stood. Heading for the door, he said, "I have a plan. Give me a few minutes to put it in motion."

Swag sat inside the interrogation room and waited for several minutes. The two-way observation mirror became transparent when a light flipped on inside. He spotted Doctor Howard and recognized the police chief from news articles. While Swag couldn't hear or understand their words, he could tell the conversation was animated.

Please Visit

http://www.authorchristopherdschmitz.com

Sign-up on the mailing list for exclusives and extras

Other ways to connect with me:

Follow me on Twitter:

https://twitter.com/cylonbagpiper

Follow me on Goodreads:

www.goodreads.com/author/show/129258.Christopher_Schmitz

Like me on Facebook:

https://www.facebook.com/authorchristopherdschmitz

Subscribe to my blog:

https://authorchristopherdschmitz.wordpress.com

Favorite me at Smashwords:

www.smashwords.com/profile/view/authorchristopherdschmitz

My Amazon Author Profile:

https://amazon.com/author/christopherdschmitz

Follow me at Bookbub:

www.bookbub.com/authors/christopher-d-schmitz

Finally, Doctor Howard coaxed the chief out of the gallery.

A moment later, Doctor Howard and Chief Bennet entered the room.

"Alright Swag," Doctor Howard said. "Tell him."

"Tell him what?"

"Everything."

Swag repeated the tale. He dumbed down some of the science and played up how verifiable their documented research was. When he was finished, Chief Bennet scowled.

"Alright, let's go," Doctor Howard said. "Don't say a word unless I say so."

Chief Bennet opened the door of the next room where Raymond waited. "You're sure about this," the chief asked Doctor Howard before entering.

"You know me," Doctor Howard said, "I can't bluff to save my life. This is the real deal."

Raymond and his lawyer stared at the new comers.

"I'm going to ask your lawyer to leave," Doctor Howard said, starting a heated argument.

"Just do it," Swag finally insisted. All eyes locked on him. "Raymond, I trust Doctor Howard. He's got a solution."

Raymond sent his lawyer to wait in the hallway, despite his many complaints.

"Alright, Doctor Lems," Doctor Howard said. "Tell us what happened."

Raymond gave an entire account, which was very similar to Swag's. The most convincing part was the repetition of dates and locations: the nuanced details that were hardest to fake.

Chief Bennet cursed and stroked his face.

"Do you want another point of view?" Raymond asked. "Jessica hasn't been with us real long, but she can further verify…"

"No… no. I believe you." Chief Bennet paced the room and made the Catholic sign of the cross. "You've got to bury this," he told Doctor Howard. "I'm retiring in six months. I don't need my city rebranded as Demon-ville or Ghost Central under my watch."

Doctor Howard asked a leading question, "Perhaps the custodian came into contact with something else… some other compound that could have triggered an episode like this?" All eyes locked on him.

A light lit behind Swag's eyes. "You said they were working on a new drug or some kind of chemical in another wing of the campus?"

Doctor Howard nodded measuredly. "We'll use as much truth as possible, like the fact that Mr. Gautreaux broke a container while cleaning. He would have had other cleaners and chemicals present on his skin. Chemicals can be nasty substances and I can think of a couple harmful interactions that might occur. A combination could create a dissociative anesthetic like phencyclidine… PCP."

Chief Bennet nodded. "You can send me the tox?"

Doctor Howard bobbed his head. I'll make sure it's on site."

"Then I'll make sure it goes away quickly on my end," the chief said. He gave each of them a steely eyed look. "Not a word about this. Ever. This was a tragedy—but purely accidental—both the official version and what we know actually happened." He looked at Doctor Howard, "And you owe me, Chandler… big time."

Doctor Howard winked. "This *was* a big one, Charlie, but given the times I've covered for you, we're more likely even by now."

The chief didn't look happy, and the professor's face was still creased with worry, but they'd found a way forward: one that would at least lead away from prosecution.

A half an hour later, the scientists were free to leave.

13.

Doctor Howard entered Swag's office with a couple tumblers and a flask. It was a small space and with Swag, Raymond, and Jessica also present, the laboratory would have been more comfortable… except that it was still cordoned off with police tape. It had been shuttered for over a week, now.

There weren't enough glasses present and Jessica dumped a lukewarm mug of coffee into the trash to let Doctor Howard pour her a dram. They were all dressed as if they were going to a funeral. They'd been called up for an official review after tabloid-level media outlets on the internet began reporting about Gautreaux's rampage with facts that hit too close to home.

"Some members of the review board must been listening to the rumor mill," Doctor Howard said, sipping his whiskey. He massaged his left arm with a wince. "I don't know who spilled the beans—probably one of the lawyers shared confidential details with an online outlet," he sighed. "Luckily the full truth about your project isn't likely to come out soon… not unless one of *you* is responsible for the leak—but I can't see that as the case. However, I suspect the University Board may try to put some distance between the situation and the science."

"What does that mean?" Jessica asked.

Raymond frowned and made a motion like he cocked a gun and put down a sick dog.

Swag nodded and thought about Jonah's constant fears that his livelihood was in peril. "How likely do you think that is?"

Doctor Howard frowned. "To be honest, it's already been decided. It's all over but the paperwork. They're going to instruct me to fire each of you and shut down the project. Your fate is already sealed."

Swag hung his head.

"All is not lost, yet," Doctor Howard insisted. "As the Department Head, I have the ability to bury your project for a little while in some of the back-channel and overflow sections of the budget. I know what your research is... how important it could prove itself for all mankind."

"You can do that?" Swag asked.

Doctor Howard raised a brow. "Do you have any idea how much bloat and waste there is in the university system? If you thought the government was bad, universities took that flag and ran with it... and it's been made easier since our government throws bags of money at it. I don't think anyone ever knows where the money really is or where it goes... only that we always need more of it."

Swag shook his head. *Money's not as scarce as they've been saying.*

"Just keep your heads down for a while and you'll be fine," Doctor Howard said. "Though we obviously can't have you operating out of the big lab for at least a year, not until this all blows over. Can you further your research without experiments?"

Swag shook his head. "Not likely. We need more data to continue the research, and that means experiments. Why?"

Doctor Howard frowned. "You'll have to figure something out. And I can't stress this enough, you have to publish something and soon—you've got to have a major breakthrough so I can go back to bat for you with the board when we officially bring you back on campus, or else it will help you to sell yourselves to a private firm. I have an in with Franklin Cuthbert's Ascent Group."

"You think Ascent would be interested in this?" Raymond said with an optimistic lilt.

Doctor Howard shrugged. "Maybe. They are always looking for innovation, and this is certainly new, and damned good science—even if it launches into the unknown."

"How long do we have?" Swag asked. "How long can you shield us and keep us on the payroll."

"At least a couple months," he motioned for them to follow, still massaging his arm. He pocketed his flask and led the way. "Barring another major catastrophe, they might begin poking around about that time… and I don't think the board can take another major upheaval. If one more thing happens, I fear half of them will quit—and that would create a lot of chaos for us in Director roles."

Doctor Howard led the way through familiar corridors and then opened a door for them. "The board will meet you in my office."

Swag tightened his lips and followed, thinking. *This feels more like a disciplinary meeting than a project review.*

14.

Doctor Howard's office was much more spacious, but it still proved too cramped with the addition of the six members of the review board.

Swag stared glassy eyed. Even if Doctor Howard hadn't forewarned them of the board's decision, it would have been obvious from the tones of the individual members. They harbored zero optimism and made no attempt to understand the data Swag and his team had gathered thus far. At least two of them seemed more concerned with his relationship with Jonah Gautreaux and any potential drug or chemical use in their experiments than with the science they had presented.

He nodded and answered when required, but Swag seemed like he was in a fugue and running on auto-pilot. Practically an automaton, Swag blinked and pushed to reassert his psyche when he felt his mind grow so passive that the drums in the darkest parts of his mind began to pound.

Swag tried to clear his mind, but they continued to thrum as he watched Doctor Howard. They seemed to match an agitated heartbeat and Swag shuddered. He physically shook his head to stop the fell beating.

He stiffened and sprang to attention once the beating stopped.

Aghast, he watched as Doctor Howard stiffened, clutched his chest, and then collapsed. The administrator pitched head over heel. Jessica leapt to his side and felt for a pulse; she shook her head.

"He's dead," she stated, riddled by shock.

Swag stood by the side of the office and watched the room descend into chaos as the university board members reacted. Eventually first responders arrived and confirmed what Jessica said. There was no heart-beat and all efforts at CPR or defibrillator use failed.

Eventually Jessica and Raymond joined Swag at his side, equally useless. In shock, they watched the EMTs position Doctor Howard on the stretcher.

Raymond was the only one still thinking clearly. He tapped his accomplices on the shoulder and bobbed his head towards Doctor Howard's desk. With everyone preoccupied with the medical emergency, Raymond flipped through the stack of binders on Doctor Howard's desk. He found the one detailing their project. It had been stamped "Discontinue" at the top.

Swag shook himself back into the real world. He spotted the set of keys Doctor Howard told him about over drinks and lifted a key off the line of hooks. Swag checked the address that was engraved onto the key chain's fob. He was certain he had the correct one. He left it hang, forever memorializing that night at pub in Swag's mind.

Discreetly, Raymond rolled up the manila folder and stuffed it down his pants.

Jessica saw Raymond's actions and whispered, "Do you really think that will work?"

Swag grimaced, but a hopeful light glinted in his eyes. "Knowing the old man, he already buried our project in administrative paperwork and those back-channels he mentioned long before he told us what he had in mind for the project." He clutched the key ring and slipped out of the office. With any luck, they'd be fine… and if they were truly lucky, Doctor Howard might still recover at the hospital once the physicians saw to him.

He looked back one time as the first responders wheeled him out the door. One of them pulled a sheet over the body.

Swag didn't think they would be so lucky.

15.

Three unlucky scientists stood outside the old home. It looked like it may have graced the cover of a Sears catalog in the 1940s when it was originally build. Swag, Raymond, and Jessica each wore their best funeral attire.

Swag and Raymond had already been moving equipment in over the last few days when they'd gotten calls from the lawyers. Thankfully it had not been the university's legal retainer but an estate attorney. Chandler Howard had phoned the lawyer after that night in the bar; he'd actually left Swag the house.

"It's gonna take a lot of work," Raymond sighed.

"Well, it's either here or nowhere," Jessica said.

Together, they stared at the house for a long, silent moment. An old ranch style with overgrown shrubs, its over-sized garage made up half the footprint meaning it was perfectly suited for their needs.

Swag raked his fingers through his hair. He turned to Jessica. "Thanks."

"For what?"

"For sticking with us. I know you didn't need to stay on, here… especially given the last couple weeks. There are many other programs out there that would be happy to have you on staff."

She waved him off. "I'm not some kinda science groupie," she grumbled. "There's lots of discovery happening here. *That's* why I'm staying, to be clear." Jessica blushed as if that were not the whole of the truth. "Besides," she held up the white lab rat, "Someone's got to look after Little Satan."

Swag patted the bulge in his pocket where the vial of illuminated goo containing the *real* Little Satan. The entity they'd been studying remained in stasis and was always kept nearby. He didn't dare risk exposing anyone else to his dark secret.

He tossed Raymond the key ring. "Well… let's get started. We need to find something worth publishing before whoever replaces Doctor Howard discovers that our program is still on the books even though it was supposed to be shuttered."

"How long do you think that will be now that Howard is gone?" Jessica asked as Raymond jiggled the key in the front door lock and coaxed the stiff tumblers to engage.

Swag shrugged. "Somewhere between six months and six years."

"I don't know how lucky a person can get," Jessica winked at him, and then held up the lab rat and spoke to him like a friendly, family pet. "Come on, then. Let's get to work."

The End begins in The Shadowless: Bloodguilt

Read a preview on the following pages!

Christopher D. Schmitz

The Shadowless

-1-

Bloodguilt

Prologue

Doctor Raymond Lems awoke with a gasp and sat up. Pain riddled his body. It forced him to drop back upon the collapsible stretcher where he found himself laying. His torso felt like someone stabbed him with burning pokers. Raymond touched his hand to his chest and looked at it with groggy eyes. *Blood.*

With great effort he lifted his head enough to glimpse his chest. Raymond cried out as he peeled away the blood-soaked gauze. *Bullet holes—and why can't I hear anything?* He could only feel an empty rattle in his throat as he screamed—tinnitus drowned out all sounds. Shock rang in his ears, drowning out everything else.

Where in the Hell am I? What happened—this is all General Braff's fault. I'm certain of it!

Raymond didn't recognize the room, though it looked familiar… these were the same color schemes company designers painted at his research lab; supposedly they calmed people. He growled. Raymond had quit the lab after finding they had begun secret experiments on children and the disabled.

Wiping away a hot tear, he tried to piece everything together, but he couldn't remember anything that had happened since meeting up with Agent Scofield at that crappy diner. "Why can't I remember?" he barely heard his voice as the ringing in his ears lessened.

He knew why he couldn't remember, but he refused to entertain such a notion. If he had become a carrier—if those *things* had controlled his body— then all hope was lost.

Even though Raymond wasn't a medical physician, he was still a doctor, and as such he recognized many of the haphazardly strewn medical supplies upon on the table next to him. A bag of blood hung on a rack; it fed into his IV and kept him from bleeding out. *Why did they leave me here? Where are the doctors and nurses?*

A second bag of fluid hung nearby—this one contained a mix with morphine in it, but it hadn't been injected yet. Shakily, Raymond pinched the catheter and rammed it into a vein. It only took a few tries. After a few seconds, the pain relaxed enough that his ears began operating again; his body fought back against the trauma and shock.

He looked over his body again, assessing the swelling and purple bruises. Some kind of noise blurped in the hallway as he looked over the bullet wound.

Who in the Hell shot me? Raymond wondered as he scanned his surroundings with fresh eyes. *And who puts a gunshot victim in a supply room?* He groaned and crawled off the bed before staggering across the linoleum. He knew the answer: *someone with no intention of coming back.*

The research scientist yanked the intravenous lines from his arms and pushed open the door where the swelling sounds of chaos greeted him. Yellow lights flashed everywhere in the hall, bathing everything with pulsating amber. Warning sirens shrieked in time with klaxon lights. Inhuman screams echoed from a nearby stairwell sounding like some kind of portal to the underworld he'd often joked that his and Swaggart's madcap research would open.

Raymond stumbled across the hall and found a door with a familiar nameplate. He scowled, but opened the entrance to General Roderick Braff's office and locked it behind him.

"Where are you, Swaggart?" Raymond limped across the hallway and towards the broken window at the far side of the room wondering where his friend had gone. Blood leaked from his oversaturated bandages and he felt light headed.

Shards of glass crunched underfoot as he meandered past the general's ornate, wooden desk. A bittersweet odor tugged at his nose. The doctor grabbed clumsily at the smoldering cigar that lay on the desktop.

With shaky fingers, Raymond barely succeeded in placing the smoking husk between his lips by the time he got to the busted window pane. He peeked out at the commotion. A herd of bodies sprinted across the far slope, heading up the hillside in a herd panic. Dread filled the researcher's gut with hot regret. It all made sense: the blackout, the gunshots, the sirens. *The entities have broken free from their containment units in the basement.*

He looked at the ground and noticed an empty shoe abandoned upon the tangle of broken, bloody glass. Raymond couldn't be certain, but he thought it could be Braff's brand. It made him happy to think that someone had finally thrown that bastard

Christopher D. Schmitz

through a second story window. He just wished it could have been there to see it.

Raymond looked back towards the mountainside. The peaks stood in stark contrast to the eerie light glowing behind them. Then, something brilliant flashed and all the light on Earth went out.

Christopher D. Schmitz

THE SHADOWLESS
- BLOODGUILT -
BOOK I
CHRISTOPHER D. SCHMITZ

THE SHADOWLESS
- THE DARK VEIL OPENS -
CHRISTOPHER D. SCHMITZ

THE SHADOWLESS
- THE WORLD BURNED -
BOOK I
CHRISTOPHER D. SCHMITZ

THE SHADOWLESS
- THE DEVIL INSIDE -
BOOK I
CHRISTOPHER D. SCHMITZ

Stay in the Light... Stay Alive...
the SHADOWLESS
HTTPS://WWW.SUBSCRIBEPAGE.COM/SHADOWLESS

About the author:

Christopher D. Schmitz is author of both Sci-Fi/Fantasy Fiction and Nonfiction books and has been published in both traditional and independent outlets. If you've looked into indie writers of the upper midwest you may have heard his name whispered in dark alleys with an equal mix of respect and disdain. He has been featured on television broadcasts, podcasts, and runs a blog for indie authors... but you've still probably never heard of him.

As an avid consumer of comic books, movies, cartoons, and books (especially sci-fi and fantasy) this child of the 80s basically lived out Stranger Things, but shadowy government agencies won't let him say more than that. He lives in rural Minnesota with his family where he drinks unsafe amounts of coffee; the caffeine shakes keeps the cold from killing them. In his off-time he plays haunted bagpipes in places of low repute, but that's a story for another time.

Schmitz also holds a Master's Degree and freelances for local newspapers. He is available for speaking engagements, interviews, etc. via the contact form and links on his website or via social media.

Help!

Thank you for reading my book! I hope it made you laugh.

Would you please take a moment to leave me a review online? Amazon, Goodreads, or anyplace else you use is an awesome start. You can also share this title with your friends on social media and requesting it via your local library will also help.

Reviews and recommendations help more than anything else out there to help spread awareness about artists and authors. I sincerely hope my stories are worth sharing with the rest of the world!

And as always, check me out online at:
www.AuthorChristopherDSchmitz.com.

Thanks for reading and sharing!

Christopher D Schmitz

SPECIAL OFFER:

Thank you so much for checking out my book! As a special bonus for you, I'd like to invite you to join my newsletter mailing list and keep up to date on the world of Shadowless and also other stories I write. I often send exclusive offers and special content to this list.

To join, simply visit this link:

https://www.subscribepage.com/shadowless

Enter your email address and you'll be added right away!

EIDOLON COMMISION

www.ingramcontent.com/pod-product-compliance
Lightning Source LLC
Chambersburg PA
CBHW021739190726
48288CB00009B/3110